Livi-Lou
and her oily yoga toes

written by:
Mika Gainacopulos

illustrated by:
Gretchen Simons ♥ Christine Ross

Livi-Lou
And Her Oily Yoga Toes

ISBN: 978-1-7321847-0-1

Published in the United States by Livi Inspiration LLC

Written by Mika Gainacopulos

Illustrations by Gretchen Simons (drawings) and Christine Ross (watercoloring)

Cover and image designs by Mika Gainacopulos

First Edition.

Sold through Amazon. Contact Liviinspiration@gmail.com for bulk discounts.

I love you Livi-Lou.
You have changed me forever.
Someday, you will understand how.

"I will always love you, forever and ever,
more than the deepest ocean and taller
than the tallest sky."

~LL

A Message for the Adults

Hi, I'm Livi-Lou's Momma. The foundation for this book began when Livi-Lou was around three. As a first time mom, I heard warnings about "the terrible two's" or "wait until they hit three." While I agree that each stage has challenges (and also magnificent opportunities), I also believe that there is a reason why a child's behavior doesn't always reflect their best self. I found that behavior challenges in Livi-Lou often existed due to her not being able to define or express what she felt, wanted or needed. With life moving quickly, I didn't always take the time to reflect on those moments, the moments when she likely needed me most. It was nearly impossible for us to move beyond the behavior challenge when I didn't take the time to listen to what she truly needed.

This book evolved after I did spend time reflecting about our relationship. I reflected about our life challenges and became aware of the "why" behind her frustration. But really, the growth of our relationship depended on my being emotionally present at home, which I found harder when I wasn't taking time for myself. I love to practice yoga; I love essential oils; I love quiet time to think. And I didn't always take the time to do what I loved because I felt guilty being away from home. When I created my own life balance—we were able to move forward.

We learned together—sometimes butting heads, sometimes crying and sometimes giggling until our tummies hurt. But as we grew—we created a stronger bond between us. We learned about each other and ourselves, and together, we both became emotionally stronger.

Livi-Lou and I started practicing yoga together as a way to connect. It became our special time together. Each night we would practice a few poses while diffusing some of our favorite essential oils as we talked about our day. We chose aromas that felt calming to us because the aromas of essential oils helped us to create memories of our time together, the time when we felt the most bonded, loved and connected.

When an aroma is inhaled, the smell (or "olfactory") center transmits the smell to be processed within the brain's limbic system, the amygdala and hippocampus. The amygdala is responsible for the feeling of an emotion and the hippocampus connects the feeling to a memory. This connection is called a "smell memory." Have you ever smelled home-cooked, sourdough bread and smiled as it reminded you of your Grandma's kitchen? This is a "smell memory," and the reason why choosing our favorite aromas was so important. We were creating memories.

In my daily life I strive to eat organic, vegetarian and GMO-free, as well as avoid contact with toxic cleaners or harmful substances. I keep dangerous products out of my bathroom cabinets, laundry room and under the sinks. My family's health and wellness is a priority. Therefore, I hold high standards for the company where I buy our personal products as the company needs to align with my health choices. For this reason, I chose Young Living essential oils, body products and household cleaners to use in my home. Their 100% purity statement, testing rigidity and distillation process leads me to trust them as my supplier for most everything I need on a daily basis. I know there are many essential oil distributors and you will choose the best company for you and your family. Young Living is the company I use. This is not a paid endorsement for Young Living but simply, what I do. If you have questions, email me at Liviinspiration@gmail.com.

For my Mom—Thank You...

Hello! My name is Livi-Lou and I am four years old. I have a lot of fun going to school, swimming and playing piano. My teachers are awesome, but sometimes I have to wait for them to finish helping another friend before they can help me. Waiting is not very fun, but my Mom says that everyone, including me, has to wait their turn.

I was confused, and sometimes scared that I wasn't the only kid who needed my teacher's help. Before I started school, my Mom and Dad were always right there to help me, and now I wasn't the only kid who needed help. Momma says the world is filled with many wonderful and unimaginably awesome things—but, if I wasn't the center of the world, I didn't understand how that was possible?

At first I thought Momma was kidding. How could I not be the center of the world? And, like most things, Momma was right. She says that it helps to understand what you are feeling if you learn how different emotions feel inside your body. She says that emotions are the initial reactions to a situation—like when I feel safe and happy when my mom is holding me tight. And feelings are how my body responds to an emotion—like when my tummy has butterflies because I'm excited that we're going to the park.

Learning to identify my emotions and feelings really did help me feel less confused about not being the center of the world. Now that I understand more, it seems less scary.

Do you sometimes feel scared?

Even though I have been working hard to understand my emotions and feelings, it is still frustrating sometimes. Yesterday, for example, my Momma let me giggle and play all day with my friends.
I had so much fun!

But today, she said that we needed to get some work done and I couldn't see my friends. I think we should have done that work yesterday and played today! I was upset Momma told me "no,"
so I threw a fit.

My Momma said that I needed to sit in a time-out until I could use my words and then we would talk about what happened. As I calmed down, she said that emotions and feelings are important, but it is how we handle them that is critical, and understanding them
is the key to handling them.

Last night when Momma and I were getting ready for bed we talked about better ways to express my feelings instead of throwing a fit. My Momma said that when she is frustrated and having a hard time understanding her feelings that she will practice yoga because yoga gives her time to think deeply, calmly and quietly. When she practices yoga she likes to put her favorite essential oil frankincense in the diffuser. She says that smelling frankincense makes her feel peaceful.

My Momma says that the smells of essential oils connect to memories in a person's brain. So now, whenever Momma smells frankincense, she feels peaceful without even having to do yoga. She calls this a "smell memory." I really like the smells of Momma's essential oils and I like how they always make me feel better. My favorite spot for Momma to place essential oils on me is on my feet because she always tickles my toes a little as she is rubbing in the oils. It is so much fun!

Last night we practiced our favorite vinyasa yoga poses together—Down Dog, Warrior 2, Extended Warrior, Reverse Warrior and Wheel while diffusing frankincense. When we were done my Momma whispered, "I am so proud of you" in my ear. It always makes me feel better to do yoga with Momma.

I know my Mom and Dad love me very much, and I always feel safe and loved in their arms. When we snuggle I can smell Momma's jasmine shampoo and Daddy's cedarwood aftershave. If I am having a rough day and don't understand my emotions, my body feels really wiggly. It's like I can't stop my wiggles. But thinking about how my Momma and Daddy smell when we snuggle helps me to feel loved—when I feel loved, I can stop my wiggles.
Do you ever feel wiggly?

I like to keep empty bottles of jasmine and cedarwood in my pocket. This way, when I am having a hard day, I can smell my pocket oils and be reminded of my Mom and Dad. I can almost hear my Momma saying how proud she is of me when I open and smell my pocket oils. I feel stronger just thinking of their snuggles.

I Am Loved!

I like to place my favorite essential oil orange on my feet just before Prayer Pose as this helps me to feel relaxed. When I bring my hands to heart center I recenter my mind and start my yoga practice. This is when I like to close my eyes and think of those special snuggles with Momma and Daddy. With my eyes closed. I take several deep breaths to clear my mind and focus on memories that make me feel happy and calm.

My Momma says that it is important to talk about how you feel because that helps you to understand why you feel that way. So, I am going to share memories of my life and how I felt at those times. Since talking helps me, I thought it might help you too. Are you sensitive like me, and sometimes feel silly, frustrated, scared or happy?

My favorite story is how my family does yoga together almost every night before bed. I think the poses are fun, especially when I am tipping to one side and trying not to fall over.

Even my doggy does yoga. I think she has better balance than I do! Isn't she cute?

I Am Sensitive!

Our first yoga pose is Down Dog. I always try to get my wiggles out in this pose before moving on because when I am wiggly it is harder to concentrate. I make a "V" shape with my body and keep my hands and toes touching the ground. Sometimes I can even touch my heels flat to the ground!

I love when my Grandma comes to visit. We get to play dress-up and pretend to cook using an essential oil called basil. When my Grandma is visiting, she reads me five books before bedtime while we snuggle in my chair. I always feel sad when my Grandma goes home, but she helps me feel stronger by hugging me tight and telling me how special I am.

I Am Strong!

This pose is called Warrior 2 and it makes me feel like I can do anything.
I pretend my arms and legs are pushing in opposite directions, like my
doggy does when I try to get her into the bathtub!
Do you have a doggy that does that too?

My Uncle is so silly! We like to play hide-and-go-seek whenever he comes to visit. I told him his hiding spots could be better. He says that he is being creative hiding under the piano because he thinks I can't see him there! Doesn't he know that I can always smell the sandalwood essential oil that he rubs on his feet (just like me!) and I can find him anywhere? My silly Uncle, you are so funny trying to hide under the piano!

I Am Creative!

This is Extended Warrior. This pose helps me stretch my side tummy
long while I extend my arm really far above my head.

I feel adventurous when I ride my brand new purple bike from Grandpa. But when Momma says that I have to put my bike away. I feel sad and start to cry. Luckily, my Grandpa knows that making hot chocolate will help me feel better. He puts a little peppermint essential oil in my hot chocolate and it is so yummy. Thanks Grampie, for making me the best hot chocolate ever!

I Am Adventurous!

This is Reverse Warrior. This pose makes me giggle because my head is upside-down and it stretches my tummy out.

I love to run with my Auntie! One time when we were running I tripped on my shoelace and fell down. I had an owie and started to cry. My Auntie is so thoughtful—she knew some kisses and a drop of *lavender* essential oil would make my knee feel better.

Two kisses later and I was back to running. I ran so fast that I beat her back to the house!

I Am Thoughtful!

This pose is called WARRIOR 3 and it is a hard pose to do but also very fun. I pretend to soar like a bird in the clouds during this pose and I giggle if I fall. It's not easy to stand on one leg!

I love to kayak with my Mom and Dad and doggy. Sometimes the waves make my kayak jumpy and I feel scared. Luckily, my Daddy holds me tightly and I laugh as his grizzly cedarwood smelling face is tickling my neck. I feel bolder and stronger knowing that he will keep me safe.

My Momma keeps my doggy safe in her kayak. I think it's funny that my doggy likes to kayak but she doesn't want to take a bath.

I Am Bold!

This is Tree Pose. I learned this pose when I was only one year old so
I've been doing it a long time by now. It's my favorite pose!

I love it when my whole family gets together for my birthday! It's like the world revolves around me and I feel very important. On my birthday my family likes to go camping, and we have a lot of fun sleeping in tents, making s'mores and going kayaking. My Mom always makes me a cake flavored with lime essential oil. Whenver I think about my birthday I get really excited and feel those butterflies flying in my tummy again.

Today I turn five! Five is such a big girl age!!

I Am Important!

This is Wheel Pose. I think it is an extra fun pose because it turns my body into a half-circle. I usually do Wheel Pose after I have done all my yoga poses on both sides and my body is warmed up.

Just like my Mommy and Daddy love me, I love my baby-doll Amelia. Before her bedtime I put my favorite essential oil orange on her feet and whisper in her ear. "I will love you forever and ever, more than the deepest ocean and taller than the tallest sky."

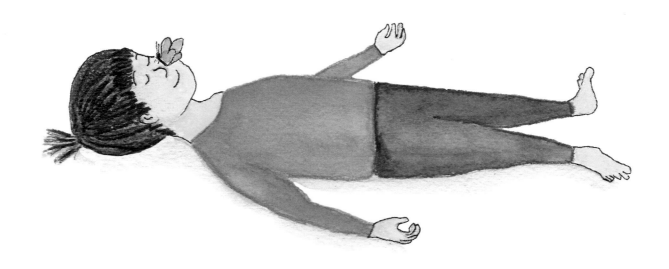

I Am Definitely Loved!

The end to my yoga practice is Relaxation Pose. By this time my mind is clear.
I feel calmer and I am no longer wiggly. Sometimes I put a little orange
essential oil on my feet right before Relaxation Pose because the oil helps
me to stay relaxed, even after my yoga practice ends.
Sometimes, I fall asleep here.
I hope I don't snore!

I Am Smart!

I Am Beautiful!

I Am Resilient!

I Am Imaginative!

I Am Awesome!

I Am Ambitious!

These are the words my Momma says to me every day. She calls them "positive affirmations." She says that affirmations are short phrases of positive words that are important to remember about yourself. I can hear her saying these affirmations whenever I smell jasmine since her words are saved in my memories and connected to the smells of the oils. I know that. . .

I Am Special!

I Am _____

What are you feeling now?

Now that I am five I don't have to wait for the teacher to help me as much anymore. My friends and I work together when we have questions and help each other when we are writing our letters or painting pictures.
Do you like my picture below?

Sometimes I still feel scared and confused. I still have rough days. My friends say that sometimes they also feel scared and confused. It makes me feel better knowing we have the same feelings. It is fun having friends and not being the center of the world. As my Momma says, when you work together you can transform the world into an even more wonderful and unimaginably awesome place.

Yoga Glossary

Vinyasa Flow

The style of yoga that I practice is called vinyasa yoga. A vinyasa is a series of yoga poses that flow together easily, has a purposeful mental intention, and is structured around a person's breathing. The action of steady breathing sustains the vinyasa's dance-like flow as each movement is connected to either an inhalation or exhalation. Vinyasa yoga is typically first practiced with one side of the body leading and then repeated on the other side.

Prayer Pose

This pose is most often performed prior to the beginning of one's yoga practice. It is a purposeful and quiet moment to create and dedicate a mental intention prior to the flow. This moment provides time to let go of negative energy and remember the personal motivation for the yoga practice. In prayer pose one is standing tall, feet touching, hands with palms together at heart center, and eyes closed. Take a few deep breaths, and with each breath, begin to relax the muscles of the face and jaw, shoulders, chest, arms, legs and feet.

Down Dog

Down dog is typically a grounding pose before moving into the flow of a vinyasa series. In down dog, the hips rise up high so the body can make a "V" shape. The hands are shoulder-width apart, palms flat with fingers wide, and the feet hip-width apart while pushing the soles of the feet downward towards the mat.

Warrior 2

Warrior 2 is a strong standing pose where the front knee is bent and toes are facing the top edge of the mat. The back leg remains straight with the foot parallel to the back of the mat. Arms are typically straight out to the sides like the letter "T" and gaze is forward-looking, over the front arm.

Extended warrior

Extended warrior maintains the same leg forward as in warrior 2 with the front knee bent, back leg straight, with the foot parallel to the back of the mat. Keeping the left leg forward, the body pivots forward at the pelvis so that the left elbow lightly rests on the left knee and the right arm straightens up towards the sky. The head turns so the eyes gaze into the upward hand. (When the right leg is forward, the body pivots forward at the pelvis so that the right elbow can lightly rest on the right knee and the left arm can straighten up towards the sky.)

Reverse Warrior

Reverse warrior maintains warrior 2 legs, but this time the torso bends away from the forward leg, opening the opposite side of the body as in extended warrior. When the left leg is forward, the right elbow is straight with the hand resting on the right leg and the left hand reaches up towards the sky. The gaze is into the palm of the top hand. (When the right leg is forward, the left elbow is straight with the hand resting on the left leg and the right hand reaches up towards the sky.)

Warrior 3

The leg that was bent in the last three poses is now straight and supports the body as the non-standing leg pushes straight backwards, forming a right angle. The non-standing foot is flexed with toes pointed downward while the arms stretch forward along the sides of the head. The body looks like the letter "T" when viewed from the side. Gaze is downward for safe head and neck alignment.

Tree Pose

The standing leg stays the same as in warrior 3 while the non-standing leg is lowered and placed so the sole of that foot rests on the inner ankle of the standing leg. Hands are brought into prayer position and gaze is lowered.

When tree pose is completed the vinyasa series on the first side of the body is completed. It is now time to repeat all the poses with the other leg in front starting in down dog and continuing through warrior 3. Once both sides are complete move into wheel pose.

Wheel

This pose begins by lying on the back, feet hip width apart and knees bent. While keeping the feet stationary, reach the palms of the hands with thumbs next to the ears until they touch the floor next to the head. Keeping the elbows pointed upwards, raise the hips high to make a half-circle shape. If the hips are raised high enough, the head will be able to relax downward and avoid neck extension.

Relaxation Pose

Lie flat on the back with palms facing upwards towards the sky. Gently straighten the legs and allow the feet to roll slightly outward. This is an excellent time to close the eyes and reflect on how the energy and mind have changed (for the better) since the beginning of the vinyasa series.

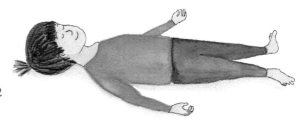

About The Author

Mika Gainacopulos fell in love with yoga in 2011 while training to run a full marathon, finishing her master's degree and balancing 4 part-time jobs! In 2012, she discovered essential oils and began exploring their potential for health and wellness. After moving to the Pacific Northwest and becoming a mother (to the very charming Livi-Lou), she has been educating others through teaching community yoga classes and sharing her knowledge of essential oils. She enjoys organic gardening and canning, camping on the beach, and traveling with her Vizsla and Livi-Lou.

She can be contacted at: https://www.facebook.com/liviinspiration/ https://www.instagram.com/yogamikagain/ or Liviinspiration@gmail.com

Stay tuned for the audio version!

Shaun -
did you think 6 yrs ago
that we would be having
doggy-dates? Haha - someday
we will have time to get
drinks again (). Thanks for
supporting me through all
my ideas......
Mika

Made in the USA
Lexington, KY
21 April 2018